# Come Hor...

Dona Herweck Rice

**Publishing Credits**

Rachelle Cracchiolo, M.S.Ed., *Publisher*
Conni Medina, M.A.Ed., *Managing Editor*
Nika Fabienke, Ed.D., *Content Director*
Véronique Bos, *Creative Director*
Shaun N. Bernadou, *Art Director*
Seth Rogers, *Editor*
John Leach, *Assistant Editor*
Courtney Roberson, *Senior Graphic Designer*

**Image Credits:** p.4 (top) eFesenko/Alamy; p.6 (top) RedNumberOne/Alamy; all other images from iStock and/or Shutterstock.

---

**Teacher Created Materials**
5301 Oceanus Drive
Huntington Beach, CA 92649-1030
www.tcmpub.com
**ISBN 978-1-4938-9872-5**
© 2019 Teacher Created Materials, Inc.
Printed in China
Nordica.082018.CA21800936

The  were

cats

in the  .

garden

Did they all come ? No.

home

The  were

cats

in the 🌳 .

tree

Did they all come

? No.

home

The  were

cats

in the  .

trash

Did they all come

? No.

home

The  were

cats

in the  .

basket

Did they all come

? No.

home

The 🐱 were

cats

in the 🌱.

grass

Did they all come

? No.

home

# High-Frequency Words

**New Words**

all come
did no
were

**Review Words**

in the
they